THE
NIGHT THE
MOON
WENT OUT

THE NIGHT THE MOON WENT OUT

SAMANTHA BAINES

Illustrated by
LUCY ROGERS

BLOOMSBURY EDUCATION
LONDON OXFORD NEW YORK NEW DELHI SYDNEY

BLOOMSBURY EDUCATION

Bloomsbury Publishing Plc
50 Bedford Square, London, WC1B 3DP, UK
29 Earlsfort Terrace, Dublin 2, Ireland

BLOOMSBURY, BLOOMSBURY EDUCATION and the Diana logo are trademarks of
Bloomsbury Publishing Plc

First published in Great Britain in 2021 by Bloomsbury Publishing Plc

Text copyright © Samantha Baines, 2021
Illustrations copyright © Lucy Rogers, 2021

Samantha Baines and Lucy Rogers have asserted their rights under the Copyright,
Designs and Patents Act, 1988, to be identified as Author and Illustrator
of this work

A catalogue record for this book is available from the British Library

ISBN: PB: 978-1-4729-9351-9; ePDF: 978-1-4729-9353-3; ePub: 978-1-4729-9352-6

2 4 6 8 10 9 7 5 3 1

Text design by Laura Neate

Printed and bound in in the UK by CPI Group Ltd, CR0 4YY

To find out more about our authors and books visit www.bloomsbury.com and sign up
for our newsletters

CONTENTS

CHAPTER 1

Aneira had a big problem.

Her bedtime had started out like it always did, reading with her mum…

"What was that word again, Mum?"

"The new word we learnt from the book?"

Aneira had nodded.

"It was 'nocturnal', darling," Mum had said.

"I like the sound of it. It is like knocking on a door and doing a turn afterwards! Knock – turn – al," Aneira had giggled.

"Do you remember what it means?"

"It doesn't mean knocking or turning. It means doing things at night," Aneira had remembered.

"Yes, well done," her mum smiled. "Some animals are nocturnal and wake up and move around at night when we are asleep."

"I wouldn't like to be nocturnal, I like the daytime," said Aneira firmly.

"Well that reminds me, as you don't want to be nocturnal, I think it's bedtime," her mum had said.

Aneira was already in bed. She was wrapped in her softest, comfiest pyjamas, the blue ones with clouds on them. She'd had a hot chocolate and she was feeling all snuggly. Outside the streets were quiet, the sun had turned in for the day and Aneira could see the dark creeping underneath her bedroom curtains.

"Mum, don't forget about my light," called Aneira.

Mum carefully reached over to the light switch. Aneira looked up to see the familiar shapes on the ceiling that shone from her night light but they didn't appear.

Mum shook her head as she tried the switch a few times but it wasn't working.

This was a big problem. It was a huge problem actually.

You see, Aneira was afraid of the dark.

She wouldn't ever tell her friends at school that she was afraid of the dark; she didn't want them to laugh at her. When they had sleepovers she always made sure she slept by the door and left the corridor light on so no one noticed. The truth was, she was really very very terrifyingly scared of the dark.

When it was dark, Aneira imagined she could hear monsters growling under her bed and ghosts going "oooooohhhh" in the corners of her room. She couldn't actually hear those things because she had hearing loss and so in the daytime she wore hearing aids, which curled around each of her ears. They had sparkly red moulds that sat inside her ears and shiny red cases that sat behind her ears. She liked them because they were colourful and could be controlled on her mum's smartphone. It was useful to be able to turn them down when everything got a bit loud.

Each night Aneira had to take her red hearing aids out and put them in a special box to charge them, just like her mum did with her tablet. She wore her hearing aids all day from as soon as she got up to just before she went to sleep. Sometimes she thought she might just wear them in her sleep too but then they wouldn't charge, plus they were a bit uncomfortable if you slept at funny angles. Aneira liked sleeping at funny angles, it made sleeping more fun.

Not being able to hear everything made the dark even scarier. Aneira worried that there were terrible warnings she couldn't hear. She imagined long ghostly fingers trying to pinch her whilst she slept and monsters trying to eat her toes. No, she could absolutely not sleep without a light.

"I want my night light," she said firmly to her mum.

Her voice sounded far away without her hearing aids on. It was as if all the sounds had run away from her, like the kids did at school when she'd first got her hearing aids.

"There's always a light in the dark sweetheart" said Mum, "just look out of your window and there's a night light there for everyone."

Mum pulled open the curtains. Aneira looked up and out of her window into the darkness. She saw a big round light shining right there in the sky.

Aneira frowned.

"I don't want the Moon, I want my night light!"

"I promise you'll be fine. Now try and get some sleep, I'll be right down the stairs if you need me," said her mum as she closed Aneira's bedroom door.

Aneira lay still in the darkness in her room. She'd never seen it so dark. There were shadows stretching across the ceiling and she started imagining all the noises they could be making. She tried squeezing her eyes shut but that didn't help either. She opened one eye and looked at the Moon out of her window. The Moon didn't light up her room like her night light did. The Moon didn't create pretty shapes on her ceiling to cover up all the strange shadows that seemed to creep towards her. The Moon wasn't able to comfort her by being right next to her head just like her night light was, it was too far away from where she lay in her bed. She didn't want the Moon, she wanted her night light in her room, just where it always was.

"I don't want the rubbish Moon," she said out loud to herself. "I want my night light."

Then just like that, the Moon went out.

CHAPTER 2

It was pitch black.

It was so dark that Aneira couldn't make out her toes at the end of her bed or even her hand in front of her face. In darkness like this she would never be able to see the monsters creeping up on her and she definitely wouldn't be able to hear them either, as her hearing aids were tucked up in their charger on the floor by her bed. She thought about reaching down to get them but as soon as she stretched her hand out, she imagined all the creepy things that could be hiding under her bed that would grab her and pull her under. She tucked her hand safely back under the duvet. She was sure a monster would grab her any minute now even through her duvet and she would have no warning.

Aneira was scared. She couldn't see anything because of the dark plus she couldn't hear anything without her hearing aids. Seeing and hearing felt like two pretty important things. She could still smell but she wasn't sure what monsters smelt like so that wouldn't be much use. Her body felt cold, even though she was lying in her warm bed. She tried to remember that her mum was just downstairs but it wasn't helping. Her shoulders started to hurt and she realised she had them pulled up around her ears in fear. She felt frozen in the darkness, like the dark had made her body as heavy as concrete and she'd never be able to move again. She needed to get to safety, so she quickly pulled her bed covers up over her head and curled up underneath them for protection.

Then she remembered to breathe. Breathing helped. It was still dark under her duvet but as she blinked a few times her eyes adjusted and she could see her hands in front of her and then her legs and her blue pyjamas. She felt a little bit safer under the duvet and so she let out a big breath which let out some of her fear too.

What had happened? Why had it got so dark?

She remembered saying she didn't want the Moon and then everything went black. Wait, had the Moon gone out? That wasn't possible, was it?

Aneira took a big breath to prepare herself and then lifted her duvet cover the smallest amount so she could peek out of the gap. It didn't seem quite so dark now and she could make out the end of her bed and the window. She looked out the window and she saw… nothing.

There had been a big white shining ball in the night sky and now there was nothing, just a blank black page. She couldn't even see any stars. Where was the Moon? Wait, had she made the Moon go out? This was not good.

She had to have a closer look; maybe the Moon was hiding. She needed to get closer. Although, getting closer also meant getting out of bed. Keeping the duvet over her head like a protective cape, she moved into a crouching position on the bed. The window wasn't too far away and if she could jump over to it she could avoid anything that might be hiding under her bed and could reach out to grab her.

She took a deep breath and silently counted to three and then jumped as close to her window as she could. Luckily, she had

soft carpet in her bedroom so her jump didn't make too loud a noise, although she couldn't really tell as she didn't have her hearing aids in. She pressed her face up against the window so it squished against the cold glass. The Moon was gone! She could see street lights over houses and then just emptiness. No Moon! What had she done?

Oh no!

There was a lamp on her windowsill, which she quickly switched on. Staying where she was, Aneira peeked out from under her duvet cape and did a monster check. Now the light was on, her room didn't look scary anymore and there wasn't anything hiding in any corners that could snatch her. Phew! She put her duvet back on the bed and turned to look back out of her window. The Moon was nowhere to be seen.

Now she wasn't scared, she was panicking instead!

She had to get the Moon back before anyone realised it was gone. She could get in a lot of trouble. In her science class they had learned that the Moon's gravity helped the sea have its tides and it also kept the Earth on its course around the Sun. What if no Moon meant no Sun? What if it meant darkness forever? She had to fix this.

She looked around her room for inspiration. Her heart was beating quickly in her chest.

This was all her fault. She looked up at the sky outside her window and it was still empty. No Moon.

What was she going to do now? Should she get her mum and explain?

No, she couldn't do that. She was sure she could fix this herself; she was ten whole years old. She would fix the Moon before anyone found out and then she wouldn't get in trouble. Aneira hated getting in trouble but it seemed to happen quite a bit without her meaning it to. Only yesterday, she had accidentally dropped one of her hearing aids in the sink which was full of water and even though she'd scooped it out really quickly, her mum had had to put it in a bag of rice to dry it out. She didn't know why rice was good at drying things out; maybe it was like a towel for phones and hearing aids. Her mum had been angry with her as hearing aids were really expensive and cost a lot to fix. Luckily her hearing aid was fine but she didn't want to make her mum angry again so soon. No, she would have to sort this out on her own, but how?

Maybe if what she'd said had made the Moon go out, she could say something else to bring it back. Surely that would work. She twisted the handle on her bedroom window as quietly as she could and opened it just a sliver. The cold night air started seeping into her bedroom, as she put her lips to the crack and said in her loudest whisper.

"Moon, I'm sorry for what I said. I do need you. Please light up again!"

She looked up at the sky but nothing had changed.

Maybe she needed to try harder, so she opened her window wider and really begged this time.

"Please Moon, I'm realllllyyyyy sorry. I promise I will be nicer to you and say that

I do need you all the time, if you just come back on."

She stared at the dark sky, crossed her fingers and hoped that it would work but nothing happened. The sky stayed dark.

Oh no!

"What are you doing, little girl?"

A voice had sprung out from the darkness and made her jump. It was a little strange as she could hear the voice loudly and clearly even though she wasn't wearing her hearing aids. It was almost as if the voice was speaking from inside her head which wasn't usually how she heard noises. She turned to see a large owl sitting on the tree next to her window.

"Oh," said Aneira as she stumbled backwards.

She peered at the owl. "Oh hello."

At least owls weren't very scary.

"Wait, owls don't talk," said a confused Aneira.

"Well I wish someone had told me that," replied the owl.

There wasn't much she could say to that so she decided the best thing to do was to be polite and answer the owl's question.

"Well… Mrs Owl, I accidentally, sort of, said that I don't want the Moon and then it went out," explained Aneira, hopping nervously from foot to foot.

She wasn't sure why she was so nervous telling the owl what had happened but it looked very wise with its large eyes and very still body and for some reason she didn't want the owl to be angry with her.

"Ahhhhh," said the Owl.

"I'm really sorry… Mrs Owl, I didn't mean to do it. I asked it to come back on and even said sorry," blurted Aneira.

"Not to worry and please call me Mrs O. Mrs Owl sounds so formal, dear."

"Oh yes, sorry… Mrs O," apologised Aneira.

Mrs O nodded her approval.

"I believe I know someone who can tell us how to get the Moon back on but we need to be quick, otherwise it might get stuck like this," said Mrs O. "You'll need to come with me, dear."

Mrs O, the talking owl, landed on Aneira's windowsill and spread her huge beautiful wings out wide. Mrs O was dark brown and caramel coloured and her feathers looked very soft up close, like a feathery brown pillow.

"Wait, what do you mean come with you?"

Mrs O turned her head round to look at Aneira but her body stayed still! Aneira worried that Mrs O's head would twist right off but instead she calmly looked at Aneira with her big yellow eyes.

"Woah!"

Aneira backed away from the window.

"Oh sorry dear, I forget that the head-turning can scare humans. I'm fine. It's actually meant to do that, it's very useful to see if anyone is sneaking up on you.

Anyway, I just wanted to tell you to climb on and I'll take you to turn the Moon back on."

Aneira just stared at the owl.

A minute ago Aneira definitely would have said that owls didn't talk and now she was having a conversation with one, without her hearing aid and it wanted her to climb on its back and fly her away. What was going on? She also realised that before tonight she definitely wouldn't have thought the Moon could go out, yet here she was.

"Hang on. You are an owl and you talk and the Moon has gone out. I know I have to fix it but we've only just met and Mum always tells me not to go with strangers," said Aneira firmly.

"Did she mention owls?"

"Well, no," admitted Aneira.

"And did she also mention what to do when you turn the Moon off and have to switch it on again quite urgently?" asked

Mrs O with her head still facing Aneira and her body facing out of the window.

"Erm… no."

"Well then, climb on my back dear. I will look after you. Don't worry, you won't hurt me, owls are very strong, especially talking ones," said Mrs O.

"Wait! There's something else."

"What is it, child?"

"It's just that… well… I guess… well, that is to say… I'm… I'm scared of the dark," blabbed Aneira.

She'd actually mostly forgotten about the dark and being scared of it in all the panic but now she was faced with a talking owl who wanted her to fly out into the very very dark night sky, all the fear came flooding back.

Mrs O blinked slowly over her pointy beak. Aneira realised that it was the first time she had seen the owl blink. Maybe owls didn't blink as much as humans. Even so, Mrs O didn't look impressed.

"It's just that it's very very dark out there, even darker than in my room without the light on," explained Aneira.

"I see," said Mrs O, thankfully sounding understanding.

Mrs O closed her wings and turned her body so that all of her was facing Aneira.

"To me, the dark is home, dear. I sleep during the day, you see. I don't know how you humans deal with all that bright light, it hurts my eyes. The day is so noisy too and the night-time is nice and quiet which makes my ears happy. We owls have very good hearing, you know."

Aneira didn't know that actually.

"I didn't know that actually. My hearing isn't very good. I wear hearing aids in the day to help me hear the teachers at school and the phone ringing and things like that. I can hear without them, but I have to concentrate a bit harder especially if there is another noise too."

Mrs O nodded.

"Ah I see. Well, I am glad you can hear me dear. Talking owls will always be heard, it is just the way of things, a special ability we have. Actually, my eyesight isn't very good with things close to me, although I'm good at spotting things far away."

"That's the same as my mum but she wears glasses."

"I tried those but they fall off when I fly," explained Mrs O.

Aneira nodded understandingly.

"You might actually love the night-time, dear. There isn't much to concentrate on hearing as it is quite quiet. I can hear mice rustling in the undergrowth a whole field away but you don't need to hear that. I find the dark very peaceful, none of that shouting and those car horns and doors slamming," said Mrs O.

Aneira stepped closer to the window to listen outside and Mrs O was right. She'd never really thought about it before but there was much less noise in the dark. She'd always imagined that the dark was scary because she couldn't hear what was going on but maybe it was quite peaceful too.

"I can show you lots of excellent things about the dark. I promise I will look after you, dear," said Mrs O, bowing her head like she was making a solemn oath.

Aneira looked up at the space where the Moon had been. She was still scared of the dark but she knew she had to fix what she'd done and Mrs O seemed nice. After all, her mum hadn't said anything about not going with talking owls.

Mrs O turned her body and her head and spread her wings again. Aneira climbed up onto the windowsill next to the owl. She had a better view through her window from up there and all she could see was a black sky which felt a little less scary with the owl sitting beside her.

"Climb on and hold on to me tightly," said Mrs O, who thankfully kept her head facing the right way this time. "My feathers should keep you warm too."

Aneira nestled into Mrs O's back. The owl's feathers were like cushions around her knees and fingers and she was surprised that she fitted perfectly in between her wings.

"Am I hurting you?"

"Not at all, dear. Now lean in close to me," said Mrs O.

A nervous Aneira buried her face into the owl's feathers as she felt Mrs O leap into the air. Aneira expected to feel like they were falling and she gripped onto the owl very tightly but she couldn't actually feel anything. Something must have gone wrong. She lifted her head from her soft feathery bed and was surprised to see they were flying!

It wasn't like being in an aeroplane at all. Flying with Mrs O was almost as if they weren't moving at all, even though she

could see the dark outlines of trees rushing
past them and feel a light breeze against her
cheeks. Mrs O wasn't flapping her wings
like the pigeons in town did to fly, she was
gliding with her wings outstretched like a
fluffy balloon caught in the wind.

"Wow," Aneira said. "Flying is awesome."

CHAPTER 3

Aneira felt surprisingly safe for someone who had just met a talking owl, climbed on its back and was flying for the first time at night – in the DARK!

"Not bad, is it?" called Mrs O over her wing.

"It's wonderful," beamed Aneira.

From Mrs O's back she gazed upwards and to either side and even though she was surrounded by the dark, the thing that she was most scared of, it didn't feel scary at all. It just felt... brilliant.

"So why don't you like the Moon, dear?"

"Oh," said Aneira, surprised. "I do like the Moon."

"I thought you said you didn't want the Moon and that's why it went out?"

Aneira could see why that would give Mrs O the wrong idea.

"Well, yes, I did say that but it was only because of my night light not working. I normally have it on every night, it makes the shape of stars on the ceiling and it makes my room brighter so I can see into all the dark corners where things might hide," explained Aneira.

"Oh dear," said a surprised Mrs O. "What things have you found hidden in the corners of your bedroom?"

"Well… I've never actually found anything hiding before. I guess it's just where things… could hide," said Aneira.

"We owls have good eyesight in the dark as long as things aren't too close, so when we get back I could check the corners of your room to see if anything is hiding if you like, dear," said Mrs O.

"You can see in the dark? Is it from eating loads of carrots?"

Mrs O chuckled at that. "Carrots?"

"Yes, my mum says that eating carrots helps you see in the dark," explained Aneira.

"We don't eat carrots, dear, and I wouldn't like to disagree with your mother but I'm not sure that is scientifically correct," said Mrs O.

Aneira nodded, it made a lot of sense as she'd been eating carrots all her life and she definitely couldn't see any better in the dark.

They didn't talk for a bit after that but it didn't feel awkward like when she was at lunch with some of the girls at school and she couldn't hear what they were saying

because of all the noise in the canteen.
It was a nice not talking bit of time.

"Mrs O, you said you knew someone
who could help us?"

"Ah yes, apologies my dear, I should tell
you where we are going, shouldn't I! I am
taking you to the Owl Parliament to speak
to our very wise owl leader who we call, well,
Wise Owl. I am sure she will know how to
bring the Moon back," explained Mrs O.

Wise Owl and the Owl Parliament
all sounded very important which made a
Aneira a little worried. After all, she was
still just wearing her pyjamas.

"Oh. Well, we do need to know how to
bring the Moon back but will Wise Owl be
mad at me for turning it off?"

"Don't worry dear, Wise Owl is very
wise, calm and always speaks very slowly
so she never gets angry. Or if she is angry,
she's probably forgotten by the time she gets

to the end of her sentence. It can be a little slow getting things done though. Once one of the young owlets accidentally fell on her head in the middle of a parliament meeting and she wasn't angry at all, although she didn't speak for an hour," said Mrs O.

"Well, I will make sure I don't fall on her head then, just in case," said Aneira firmly.

Mrs O chuckled and nodded at that.

They glided over a forest and it looked like the rows of trees went on forever. Looking at the forest from above made Aneira think of a furry sea and she tried to imagine all the animals that were scurrying around in the furry darkness beneath them.

"Mrs O, will there be other owls at the Owl Parliament?"

"Yes dear, there will be other owls there. We meet most nights and anyone who has anything to ask Wise Owl will be there waiting to hear her advice. It takes rather a long time so hopefully they will let us jump the queue," explained Mrs O. "I usually nap whilst I am waiting."

They flew over a hilly area and Aneira spotted a river splitting the sea of trees in two.

"This is the forest of the Owl Parliament," said Mrs O after they had crossed the river. "Do you see that very large old tree in the distance?"

Aneira could see one tree that was taller and larger than the rest. It was poking its head above the others.

"That tree is hundreds of years old, dear. It is where we meet each night and where our Owl Parliament has always met. It's also where I have had some excellent naps," said Mrs O.

Aneira still didn't understand exactly what an Owl Parliament was and why they had to meet in a very old tree but it didn't seem a very good time to ask. Mrs O said they asked Wise Owl advice so maybe it was a bit like asking her favourite teacher, Mrs Allen, for help with her homework, although she was pretty sure owls didn't have homework.

"Once we land, stay still and I will explain why we are here," said Mrs O. "Hopefully they will let us jump to the front of the queue for Wise Owl's time."

"OK," said a very nervous Aneira as the very large, very tall tree got closer and closer.

The tree's branches were huge. They spread out at different heights like a very tall building with lots of different levels. Mrs O flew into the darkness of the tree and Aneira felt a jolt as they landed on one of its huge branches. She blinked a few times to help her eyes adjust. If anything, it was even darker in the tree than it had been in the night sky. She remembered what she had been told and stayed still as Mrs O began to hoot their arrival.

Up until then Mrs O had only spoken, so hearing her hoot was a bit of a shock. It was even more of a shock when Aneira heard other hoots replying to her from the tree's darkness.

Once the hooting stopped, two yellow eyes appeared in front of them, then two more above them and then all of a sudden everywhere she looked there seemed to be pairs of yellow eyes staring at them. Aneira tightened her grip on Mrs O and buried her head in Mrs O's feathers for safety. This is exactly what she had imagined was hiding in the darkness of her bedroom.

Aneira could hear more muffled hooting from around her and she was suddenly worried that she hadn't brought her hearing aids and wouldn't be able to hear the Owl Parliament at all. Just as she was beginning to panic, she heard a chuckle and then a careful but strong voice said:

"Welcome."

Just like with Mrs O, it was as if the voice was coming from inside Aneira's head and she could hear the words perfectly. It would be so much easier if humans could speak this way too, then she wouldn't feel so left out all the time. She lifted her head from Mrs O's back and saw that hanging lanterns had now been lit and were dangling from every available tree branch, giving the old tree a friendly glow. Aneira admired the tree's red-brown bark and flat cloud-shaped leaves. She gazed down and could see layers of branches beneath them with even more lanterns and green leaves sprouting from them. It was quite a beautiful tree. Then she noticed the owls. All around them on the large tree branches were rows and rows of different coloured owls. At the centre of the tree, in a hollow in its trunk, sat a very large and very old-looking owl. The owl must have been twice the size of Mrs O and its feathers were grey in places. On its head it had a crown of leaves and berries like it was the queen of the forest.

"I'd like you to meet Wise Owl," said Mrs O.

CHAPTER 4

Aneira stepped off Mrs O's back onto the branch they had landed on, in the very old tree where the owls held their Owl Parliament. The tree branch was about as wide as her bed at home and felt very solid even though they were so high up. Aneira bowed quickly towards Wise Owl. She didn't know if you were meant to bow at Owl Parliament but she knew people bowed when they met the human queen, so it seemed like a good idea.

Wise Owl chuckled.

"Welcome…

    my…

        child…

            to…

                the…

                    Owl…

                        Parliament."

Mrs O was right, Wise Owl did speak
very slowly! This could take a while.

"I have explained our problem and that the Moon has gone out," said Mrs O.

That must have been what all the hooting had been about. Aneira was relieved as explaining what had happened all over again plus how slowly Wise Owl seemed to talk might have meant it would be morning before they actually found out how to turn the Moon back on!

Aneira turned to Wise Owl.

"Yes, I am very sorry about the Moon but Mrs O said you might be able to help and tell us how to get the Moon back on?"

"Yes… I… know… how… to… bring… the… Moon… back… on."

Aneira found herself hopping on the spot with impatience as Wise Owl spoke.

"But… first… I… must… finish… the… last… owl's… question."

So Mrs O hadn't got them to the front of the queue then. She hoped this question didn't take too long.

"Come," said Wise Owl to a small owl the colour of lightly toasted bread.

The small owl flew forward and said in a very high-pitched voice, "My question is about the fact that most owls only come out at night-time. I love sleeping in the day and flying at night. I have noticed that there are other animals who live like us too. I just wondered if there was a way of describing animals like us who wake up at night?"

"Ah... yes... young... one... an... interesting... question."

Wise Owl paused to think.

"This is taking too long," thought Aneira.

She knew she wasn't an owl and Mrs O had been very kind to help her try to fix the Moon but if they didn't find out how to do that soon, she was going to be in a lot of trouble. Aneira thought back to the book she'd been reading with Mum before bed.

"Nocturnal," Aneira muttered.

Mrs O turned to her. "Did you say something, dear?"

"Nocturnal," Aneira said louder. "That is the word for animals who sleep during the day and wake up at night."

The small toast-coloured owl looked at Aneira and jumped up and down in excitement.

"Knock-turn-al," said the small owl, trying out the word.

"This… is… correct." Wise Owl confirmed.

"Thank you, thank you," said the small owl and flew back to its place on a lower branch.

Aneira smiled and suddenly felt much more confident.

"Excuse me, Wise Owl. I wondered if we could ask our question now as it's quite important. I think Mrs O has explained that

I accidentally made the Moon go out. We were hoping you could tell us how to turn it back on," said Aneira boldly.

There was a moment of silence and Aneira wondered if she'd done the wrong thing. She hoped Wise Owl wouldn't be angry and would answer her question. After all, she definitely hadn't fallen on Wise Owl's head.

After a moment, Wise Owl opened her beak to speak.

"You… must… take… a… journey… to… the… Moon… itself.

Only… the… one… who… caused… the… Moon… to… go… out… can… be… the… one… to… bring… it… back."

Aneira was confused. "But how do I bring it back and how do I land on the Moon?"

"You… do… not… need… to… land… on… the… Moon.

You… need… to… get… close… to… the… Moon."

"But what do we do when we get there? How can I turn it back on?"

"The… Moon… is… a… night light… it… can… be… turned… on… like… any… light.

You… must… go… quickly.

The… Moon… must… be… back… on… before… dawn… or… it… may… be… lost… forever."

The other owls started hooting and flapping their wings in agreement.

"Right. Well, that was sorted much quicker than I expected. Climb on my back dear, it is time for us to go," said Mrs O.

"But what about the Moon? We still don't know exactly how to get it back on," blurted Aneira.

"Wise Owl will always tell an owl

exactly what they need to know. If these are her instructions, we must follow them," said Mrs O.

Aneira climbed onto Mrs O's back as Wise Owl closed her eyes and the other owls carried on hooting in encouragement. Even without her hearing aids, Aneira found it all a bit loud. It reminded her of sports day at school. Maybe she could convince Mrs Allen to add a flying on the back of an owl race next year. That was a race Aneira might actually have a chance of winning.

"Don't worry, dear," said Mrs O more quietly now, "Wise Owl gave us a clue in what she said, we just need to work it out. Now hold on tightly."

With Aneira safely on her back Mrs O took off and they both left Wise Owl and the hooting Owl Parliament behind them.

CHAPTER 5

Aneira reached a hand out into the
darkness and felt the air running through
her fingers like very soft sand. They were
flying through the night sky again. Aneira
thought about all that had happened so
far this evening and how it had all started
from being afraid of the dark. It was strange
that you could be scared of something that
you couldn't actually touch or hear, like
darkness. Up there with Mrs O, the dark
didn't feel creepy; instead it felt far away
and like it couldn't hurt her. Come to think
of it, the dark couldn't hurt her or anyone.

She'd never thought of it like that before. After the noise of the Owl Parliament it was pretty peaceful up in it too.

Mrs O flapped her wings beneath Aneira as they climbed higher.

"Wise Owl told us to get close to the Moon but I still don't know how I can turn it back on," said a worried Aneira to Mrs O.

"We still have a bit of a journey to get to the Moon dear, so we have time to work that out," soothed Mrs O.

"Yes I suppose," agreed Aneira.

"As we are making the journey, we might as well enjoy ourselves," said Mrs O mischievously. "If you feel brave enough, look down. I think everything looks rather wonderful from up here."

Aneira held on tight and looked down. They were much higher in the sky and everything was so small. The forest looked like a furry doormat from up here and the cities looked like little houses in a toy village. The street lights left patches of yellow on the dark grey outlines of tiny roads and cars and buildings; it looked a lot like a painting in a museum they'd been to on a school trip.

All the houses began to disappear completely and she could see trees and large

flat squares like a patchwork blanket. Then something else large and flat and dark but she couldn't see its edges. Every so often there were little white lines that came and went like froth.

"The sea!"

"Yes, dear," said Mrs O.

The sea looked so different in the dark. It was quite still and looked more like a swimming pool filled with black water. All of a sudden, Aneira could smell the salty air too.

"I want to show you one of my favourite views at night," said Mrs O.

As they flew along the edge of the sea, Aneira could see a light coming from up ahead but it looked like it was coming from inside the water. It didn't look like the streetlamps and house lights she had seen earlier that were yellow splashes. This light was blue and it was spattered along the shoreline in patches.

"Wow! What is that?"

"It is something called plankton, which are small insect-like creatures that live in the water and can light up at night."

"It's beautiful," said Aneira as they flew over a huge area of the blue light.

It looked a lot like a galaxy that Mrs Allen had shown the class in science which was blue and made up of lots of different stars and planets shaped in a pattern.

"Just think, these tiny plankton have been lighting up like this for years and years, before there were streets and houses and cars. They were the first light in the dark," said Mrs O.

"Wow," said Aneira again. It was pretty amazing and there were no light switches in sight.

"Do you know the other original light in the dark?"

"Erm…" said Aneira thinking hard.

"Stars and… the Moon, dear," reminded Mrs O.

Oh yeah. She had almost forgotten that she had made the Moon go out and that was the real reason she was flying through the dark on the owl's back.

"Yes, the Moon. We need to get that back on," agreed Aneira.

"Then you'd better look up dear, we are getting closer," directed Mrs O.

Aneira was so busy looking down at the sea that she looked up and was shocked at the view. There was a whole world of light overhead. It was like they were flying in the middle of two worlds below and above.

"I can see stars!"

Aneira could see hundreds of them, like houses hanging from the sky with their bedroom lights on.

Mrs O chuckled.

"I remember when I was young, sitting in our nest, glimpsing the stars and wishing I could fly up here and see them. That was the first thing I did dear, once I got my wings working, now I only pop down to rest and catch food," said Mrs O.

Aneira thought for a moment. "What is it like to have wings?"

Mrs O chuckled again. "Well, it's rather normal I suppose. They help me fly and flying is the best way to get around. You humans spend a lot of time on roads but up here there are no roads to follow so you can choose to go wherever you like."

"That does sound kind of great," agreed Aneira.

"What's it like to have arms with no feathers and those funny hands hanging off them?"

"I haven't really thought about it before. Hands are useful, they mean I can plait hair and tie my laces and use my mum's tablet. Arms are just… quite heavy really," answered Aneira.

"Arms sound awful," said Mrs O.

"Well, they are good for lifting things and keeping jumpers on too," said Aneira.

"Owls don't wear jumpers," said Mrs O.

That made Aneira giggle.

CHAPTER 6

They flew higher and higher, between the stars, into the gap where the Moon had been. Aneira's house was a tiny speck far away and all around Aneira and Mrs O was a sea of darkness with stars like tiny pen marks. Up here, the darkness felt heavier but not like arms – more like a blanket that made Aneira feel calm.

As they got closer, Aneira worried more and more about what she would do when they got there. Mrs O said that Wise Owl had given them all the information they needed but she still hadn't told them exactly what to do. Aneira thought back to the Owl Parliament and what Wise Owl had said.

"The... Moon... is... a... night... light. It... can... be... turned... on... like... any... light."

But what did that mean?

Then...

Aneira spotted a white line running down from the darkness above them. She rubbed her eyes thinking it might be a collection of stars but no, it was definitely a line and it was getting closer.

"We are almost there, dear," said Mrs O.

Aneira looked around her at the darkness.

"But I can't see the Moon," she said.

"Of course not, its light has gone out. We need to switch it back on," said Mrs O.

Aneira looked around again, confused. Switch it on? Hang on! It was a night light. That is what Wise Owl had said. Every

night light had a switch to turn it on and off, maybe the Moon was no different!

The line in the sky seemed to be getting closer. As Mrs O flew them nearer and nearer it was looking more and more solid. It almost looked like…

No it couldn't be, could it? It looked like… string.

"Of course!" cried Aneira. "The Moon has a switch and it's a piece of string, like the light in my bathroom at home. I pull the string, there is a click and the bathroom light comes on!"

"Yes, dear. That must be it! Oh, I knew you would work it out. Wise Owl always gives us exactly the information we need," said Mrs O.

"I can see the string, Mrs O," called Aneira. "Do you think you can get me right next to it?"

"I will get you as close as I can. All you need to do is reach out, grab the string, pull down on it and then let go. You are the only one who can switch it back on, Aneira. Wise Owl said that it had to be you. Can you do it, dear?"

Aneira looked at the darkness below and now it just seemed like a really long way to fall.

"Yes I can do it," gulped Aneira.

"I am glad you said that, as we owls would really like the Moon back on. Also, I am afraid I would tip you off my back if I tried to pull the switch and we don't want that," explained Mrs O.

"No, I'd like to stay on your back I think," said a nervous Aneira.

The string was getting much closer now.

"We are almost there dear, just remember to pull down hard and then let go straight away," reminded Mrs O.

The owl swooped towards the string. Aneira held her arm out ready to grab it, although it was rushing towards them rather fast. She opened her hand to clasp the string and lent towards it. Aneira felt a rush of wind on her face.

"Did I get it?"

"I can't see the Moon dear, so I don't think you did," said Mrs O.

Aneira couldn't see the string anymore and then she realised something.

"Oh, I think I closed my eyes as we got close," admitted Aneira.

"Well dear, I know human eyes aren't as good as owl eyes but I do think keeping them open will help."

"Yes sorry," said Aneira.

That had been a silly mistake! Keeping her eyes open was definitely a good idea.

"I will circle round and come back. Remember: eyes open," prompted Mrs O.

This time, Aneira kept her eyes open and she stretched out her arm and grabbed the string!

"I got it!" she cried.

Aneira held on tightly to the string in celebration. She was so pleased that she had managed to grab it this time. She looked down and realised Mrs O was moving a lot more than usual underneath her.

"Aneira!"

The owl's body was swooping away from her! She held on tightly to the string and to Mrs O.

"Aneira, I can't stay still and hold you up!"

"Ahhhhhh," cried Aneira as Mrs O's body tipped underneath her.

Aneira looked down and was suddenly very very terrifyingly scared. It was a very long way down in the dark, nowhere near her house and her mum.

"I don't want to fall," cried a terrified Aneira.

"Pull down and let go," shouted Mrs O flapping and lurching around trying to keep them up as Aneira was holding onto the string which was holding them still.

"You have to pull down and let go or you will fall," shouted Mrs O again.

Aneira could feel her shoulders hurting

as they tensed around her ears and her body going cold. She was so frightened. She held onto the string tightly and suddenly pulled down hard and then let go.

Mrs O immediately stopped flapping and lurching but Aneira couldn't see anything. She realised that she had let go of the string because she had heard a very loud click and then she had buried her face in the owl's back.

She couldn't normally hear things like clicks of lights and the beeps of alarms but she heard this click, even without her hearing aids.

Aneira noticed that they didn't seem to be falling, which was a relief so she lifted her head from Mrs O's back and opened her eyes.

There was a lot of light. So much light that she couldn't see anything. Aneira lifted her hand up to cover her eyes.

"Oh," Aneira cried, "what is that?"

Mrs O flapped her wings once and brought them away from the blinding light.

"You can look now, dear," said Mrs O.

Aneira took her hands away from her eyes and blinked a few times. There in front of them was the Moon! It was huge this close and she could see all of the patterns on the Moon's surface, like looking into a marble with colours inside. Wow.

"The Moon! It's back!"

"Yes dear, you turned the Moon back on. Although I was worried for a minute that we might be hanging off that string forever or that you'd fall," said Mrs O.

"Yes, sorry about that, I shouldn't have held on for so long," said Aneira, realising that she hadn't followed Mrs O's instructions.

She'd been so scared that she would fall, way more scared than she'd ever been of the dark. She'd loved her adventure with Mrs O but she definitely wanted to be safe on the ground again.

"We did it Mrs O," said Aneira.

"You did it and you were very brave too," replied Mrs O.

Brave! She'd never really felt brave before but she'd been in her room in the pitch black and she'd flown through the dark night sky and she'd met a talking owl and flown on its back to visit the Owl Parliament and then she'd worked out how to turn the Moon back on, so maybe she was brave. She had never been so pleased to see the big ball in the sky.

"Oh thank you Mrs O. Thank you, thank you!"

Aneira wrapped her arms around the owl and hugged her.

"Oh my dear, you are welcome," said a happy Mrs O.

"You saved me. Thank you for coming to my window, I couldn't have done it without you!"

"Well that bit is true as you can't fly due to your heavy arms. However, I was very pleased to help dear. After all, the Moon is rather important," said Mrs O.

"It's very important. It's my night light," said Aneira smiling at the Moon.

"Well yes, among other things," said Mrs O. "All this adventure has got me rather hungry. Back to bed for you I think and then I can catch my dinner."

"It has been an adventure. An adventure in the dark and I enjoyed it, apart from the nearly falling bit. I never thought I would enjoy being in the dark but I did," admitted Aneira.

"Yes, the night can be rather brilliant, can't it?"

"Yes," said Aneira, letting out a big yawn.

She held on tightly to Mrs O, as the owl swooped back down towards the trees and the houses, guided by the light of the Moon. As they flew lower and lower, Aneira could see her house getting larger and larger, and her open window inviting her in.

It seemed like no time at all until Mrs O landed gently on her windowsill. Aneira could see her bed waiting in the middle of her dark room and it looked very peaceful and snuggly. She crawled off the owl's back and down onto her fluffy carpet.

She yawned again. She was so very tired all of a sudden.

"Thank you Mrs O, for helping me turn the Moon back on and for showing me that the dark is just as good as the light. Night-time without my hearing aids definitely isn't as scary as I thought and talking owls are pretty great even when they talk really slowly."

"You are welcome, my dear Aneira. Now off to bed please and no more turning the Moon off, if you don't mind," said Mrs O.

"I promise. Goodnight Mrs O."

"Goodnight, dear," said the owl.

Aneira turned towards her bed with another yawn.

"Wait. Will I ever see you again?"

But Mrs O had already swooped off into the night.

"I hope so," Aneira said out loud.

She closed her window and crawled into bed, her arms heavy with sleep. She looked out at the Moon and smiled just before she closed her eyes and fell fast asleep.

READING ZONE!

WHAT DO YOU THINK?

Aneira was frightened of the dark because she imagined lots of bad things when she did not have her hearing aids in. Do you think that she is still afraid of the dark at the end of the story? Think about your reasons for your answer.

Have you ever been afraid of the dark? If so, what things made you feel frightened? What did you do to help yourself not be afraid of the dark?

READING ZONE!

QUIZ TIME

Can you remember the answers to
these questions?

• What does Aneira thinks her friends
at school would do if she told them
she was afraid of the dark?

• What made the dark even scarier
for Aneira?

• Who is Aneira's favourite teacher?

• How does Aneira know the answer
to the small owl's question?

• Why did Aneira not manage to turn
the moon on at her first try?

READING ZONE!

STORYTELLING TOOLKIT

The author uses a lot of speech to help tell the story and to give us an idea of the way the characters speak.

Look back through the text and find some examples of where the author has used layout and punctuation to help the reader understand how the character is speaking. Which ones do you think are effective?

Can you think of other ways you could use layout to help show how words are being spoken by a character?